How Well Do You Know Jerry ... and His Friends?
A Trivia Book

by

Artie Mangravito

DORRANCE PUBLISHING CO., INC.
PITTSBURGH, PENNSYLVANIA 15222

All Rights Reserved

Copyright © 1998 by Artie Mangravito
No part of this book may be reproduced or transmitted
in any form or by any means, electronic or mechanical,
including photocopying, recording, or by any information
storage and retrieval system without permission in
writing from the publisher.

ISBN # 0-8059-4177-0

Printed in the United States of America

Second Printing

For information or to order additional books, please write:
Dorrance Publishing Co., Inc.
701 Smithfield Street
Third Floor
Pittsburgh, Pennsylvania 15222
U.S.A.
1-800-788-7654
Or visit our web site and on-line catalog at *www.dorrancepublishing.com*

Dedication

To Mom and Dad–thanks.
Love, A.J.

1) To pay Kenny Banya for the Armani suit, Jerry took him to what restaurant?

2) The name of the racquet that Elaine lent to a friend was?

3) What was the name of the closefitting garment that Kramer invented?

4) On what did Elaine expose her nipple?

5) What is Kramer's mother's name?

6) What was the name of the cologne that Calvin Klein stole from Kramer?

7) The name of the cartoon character displayed on Jerry's Pez dispenser was?

8) Name the two clubs at which Jerry does his stand-up act?

9) George's parents' names are?

10) Who is Jerry's comic book hero?

11) Jerry hadn't vomited since June 29, 1980, until he ate what at the bakery?

12) Name of the standby diner the gang goes to instead of Monk's?

13) Jerry's parents' names are?

14) Jerry owed twenty years worth of fines to the library for what book?

15) What was the name of the publishing company for which Elaine worked?

16) What was on the vanity plates Kramer got from the Department of Motor Vehicles?

17) What is Uncle Leo's wife's name?

18) For whom does cousin Jeffrey work?

19) For what reason did George get fired from Pendant Publishing?

20) What is Elaine's roommate's name?

21) Jerry's telephone numbers are?

22) What did George pull out of the whale's blowhole?

23) What did Jerry tell Elaine the original title of War and Peace was?

24) What was the name of Jerry's favorite tee shirt?

25) On what talk show did Kramer promote his "Coffee Table Book"?

26) How did George try to change the course of his life?

27) What did Elaine buy at the theater after she learned her boyfriend was in a car accident?

28) What illness did Jerry tell the mall security police he had when he was caught peeing in the parking garage?

29) What does Jerry change on all his new pants?

30) What is George's ATM code?

31) Kramer sells his suit in a department store for three hundred dollars to whom?

32) How much were Jerry and George paid for writing the script for their NBC pilot?

33) What did Tim Whatley give Jerry for the Super Bowl tickets?

34) What board game were Kramer and Newman playing that had to be left at Jerry's for him to watch?

35) What did Elaine call Tim for giving Jerry the same gift she gave him?

36) What did Jerry throw in the trash that Uncle Leo picked up?

37) Who did Kramer see in Dinky Donuts?

38) What happened to George when he went to the masseuse?

39) What was the idea Jerry and George pitched to NBC for a television show?

40) Bob Cobb, the gang's friend and musical conductor, likes to be called what?

41) What was it that bothered George at Susan's uncle's store?

42) Who burned down Susan's father's cabin and how?

43) Whose telephone number did Kramer leave in the pocket of the suit he sold?

44) What was left after the fire at Susan's father's cabin?

45) What is the brand name of the bike in Jerry's apartment?

46) How much did Nana put in Jerry's birthday card every year?

47) Who did George get to appear on the PBS pledge drive?

48) How does Mr. Pitt eat his Snickers candy bar?

49) To what religion does George convert for his girlfriend?

50) What does Jerry find in his girlfriend's medicine cabinet that disturbs him?

51) What is the name of the Chinese restaurant where the gang eats?

52) What is the problem with Noreen's (Elaine's girlfriend) boyfriend Dan that bothers everybody?

53) What did Jerry and Elaine find strange about the man they saw with Frank Costanza in the city?

54) What float did Mr. Pitt man in the Macy's Day Parade?

55) How did Kramer pay off his airport gambling debt?

56) What article of clothing of Jerry's did the dry cleaner wear to the movies?

57) Why does Duncan Meyer dislike Jerry?

58) What is Elaine's address?

59) Which television show does Jerry secretly watch?

60) What did Jerry hide in a napkin at Holly's apartment?

61) What did Kramer do with the Yankees autographed birthday card he took from George?

62) What ballplayer needed to hit two home runs in a game to help Kramer get the birthday card back?

63) Who was the birthday card intended for?

64) What alias did Kramer use to audition for the "Jerry" pilot?

65) George accuses the actor playing the part of Kramer of stealing what?

66) Russell Dalrymple, the NBC executive, shows up where after being rejected by Elaine?

67) What does Elaine find in Jerry's couch while watching the NBC pilot?

68) What does Joe Davola yell while attending the NBC pilot?

69) What is the name of the company George made up to continue his unemployment insurance?

70) Name the date and the teams that played the day Kramer and Newman were spit on?

71) What is Jerry's home address?

72) For what reason did Elaine stop dating Keith Hernandez?

73) Who really spit on Kramer and Newman at the ballpark?

74) What did Elaine find in the armoire that Kramer got for her?

75) Where do George's parents live?

76) What does Jerry unknowingly agree to with the low-talker?

77) Who hosted the "Today Show" when Jerry wore the "Puffy" shirt?

78) Who won the celibacy contest among the gang?

79) What does Jerry call a male bimbo?

80) In what sport do George and Kramer join Tony?

81) Who does Jane, Jerry's girlfriend, turn out to be?

82) What is Jerry's ATM code?

83) What is the name of the maitre d' at the Chinese restaurant?

84) How many years was it before the gang found out Kramer's first name?

85) Name of bookstore where Jake Jarmel held his book signing was?

86) Where did Jake Jarmel buy his eyeglasses?

87) Which one of the gang turns out to be the scofflaw?

88) To whom does Elaine give the eyeglasses that are just like Jake's?

89) What does Jimmy call his exercise sneakers?

90) What did Jerry find in the dentist's waiting room that upset him?

91) Why did Jerry put his parents up in the Waldorf Astoria Hotel?

92) How did Jerry get fleas in his apartment?

93) How does Jerry determine when someone is in love?

94) Which character wasn't on the first show?

95) What is Elaine's middle name?

96) What does Jerry say when someone sneezes?

97) How many times does Jerry estimate he had sex with Elaine?

98) What is Bab's, Kramer's mother, favorite drink?

99) What is the impenetrable chamber called where Jerry keeps his secrets?

100) What is the name of the book the real Jerry Seinfeld wrote?

101) What is the name of the bookstore where Jerry held his book signing?

102) What magazine was George reading when his mother caught him "pleasing" himself?

103) What is Elaine's sister's name?

7

104) What technique did George use to break up with Susan?

105) What is the name of the owner of the Comedy Club?

106) What did Pat Buckles ask Jerry to hold for him for a couple of months?

107) The name of the movie the gang ended up seeing instead of *Checkmate* was?

108) Where is the Comedy Club located?

109) Who was the only one who ended up seeing *Checkmate*?

110) What was stuck in George's teeth when he went on a job interview?

111) Who did Kramer punch in the nose while at the baseball fantasy camp?

112) Who did the used-car salesman tell George previously owned the LeBaron?

113) What was the name of the Chinese delivery boy who Elaine knocked down in the street?

114) What nickname does Jerry have for George when he acts dopey?

115) What was in Jerry's mailbox that Babu Bhatt needed?

116) What television sitcom was Kramer on while in L.A.?

117) What did the airport security guard find in George's bag?

118) Who did Kramer give his movie treatment to in an L.A. coffeehouse?

119) What was the name of the housemaid at the L.A. hotel where Jerry and George stayed?

120) What special request did George make of the housemaid?

121) What was the name of the movie treatment Kramer wrote while in L.A.?

122) What soap opera did Kramer work on as a stand-in?

123) What was the name of the cashier at Monk's?

124) What comparison did Jerry give for a woman having breast implants?

125) What are the supers' names in Jerry's building?

126) What did George do at his girlfriend's family's wake that offended them?

127) What did the gang buy "The Drakes" for a wedding gift?

128) What did the wheelchair-girlfriend call Kramer when she broke up with him?

129) What were some of the nicknames for Jerry when he was growing up?

130) What fell into a man's stomach during an operation that Jerry and Kramer were watching?

131) What name did George pick if he were to become a porno star?

132) How does George describe not having any control in a relationship?

133) What movie did Jerry and his girlfriend make out during?

134) Where does Kramer buy his used clothes?

135) How does Jerry describe shrinkage in a man's privates?

136) What is the name of Jerry's barber?

137) What level of education did Kramer reach?

138) What was the nationality of the woman Frank Costanza had an affair with during the war?

139) George slid into who during a softball game?

140) What musical cast members played softball against Jerry and the Improv group?

141) For what reason did Uncle Leo owe Jerry's mother fifty dollars for over fifty years?

142) What was the name of the neighbor who lived next to Nana, Jerry's grandmother, forty-five years ago?

143) Who peed on Jerry's couch?

144) What did Poppie say to Elaine which upset her and thus made her and Jerry decide to leave his restaurant?

145) What idea did Kramer have for Poppie's restaurant?

146) How did George's hand modeling come to an end?

147) What movie did George watch instead of reading the book for the book club?

148) What strange habit does George have when he goes to the bathroom?

149) What is it about the circus that Kramer doesn't like?

150) Why is George afraid of Elaine and Susan becoming friends?

151) What's the pool guy's name at the health club to which Jerry belongs?

152) How many times does Elaine estimate she and Jerry had sex?

153) What is the bubble boy's name?

154) What did Kramer save from the burning cabin?

155) What is the name of the man Babs went out with and who owns the jacket that Kramer wants?

156) What is the secret of the jacket that Kramer wants from his mother's ex-boyfriend?

157) What hand gesture does Jerry think should be used to describe homosexuals?

158) What was the storyline of the "Jerry" pilot?

159) What does Kramer request whenever he orders Chinese food?

160) The name of Susan's gay girlfriend was?

161) What video was George returning when he met Susan and her gay girlfriend?

162) What was the year and make of the B.O. car?

163) The name of the character Kramer played on the "Murphy Brown" sitcom was?

164) What team logo was on the baseball cap Elaine refused to remove while at a Yankees game?

165) What year did Jerry and George graduate from high school?

166) Of what television show is Jerry proud to say he never watched an episode?

167) How did Susan lose her job with NBC?

168) Why did Jerry's father throw away the wallet that was given to him for his birthday?

169) The name of the off-off Broadway play George said he wrote was?

170) What was the name of the school at which Jerry and George met?

171) To whom and why did Kramer relinquish his prize jacket?

172) Name of the obnoxious dog a drunken air traveler left with Jerry to watch was?

173) What did Kramer model for the Calvin Klein people?

174) The name Kramer says he would give a child of his?

175) On whom did Susan, George's girlfriend, have a crush?

176) What kind of cookies did George want to steal from an L.A. police car?

177) What was Elaine's job description at Pendant Publishing?

178) What did Jerry give to Elaine for her birthday after they began dating again?

179) Elaine's favorite movie is?

180) How did the gym teacher mispronounce George's name?

181) What is Jerry's biggest fear of being blind?

182) How does the maitred' at the Chinese restaurant mispronounce George's name?

183) What did the L.A. housemaid throw away that upset Jerry?

184) What did Elaine spray in Crazy Joe Davola's face?

185) What type of basketball player does George describe himself as?

186) Tallest woman Jerry ever slept with was?

187) Jerry's favorite explorer is?

188) Jerry gets upset when Keith Hernandez asks him to do what?

189) The high school gym teacher's teeth remind George of what?

190) The guys call underwear pulled over the head what?

191) Name of the Scotch liquor Jerry keeps in his apartment?

192) The original name of the diner where Jerry and friends ate was?

193) Whose voice causes Kramer to have seizures?

194) Why did Kramer move to L.A.?

195) What was Elaine talking about that caused the virgin to run out of Jerry's apartment?

196) What caused Kramer to call out the name Yo Yo Ma?

197) Jerry's reasoning for not being a leg man?

198) Kramer's first name is?

199) What other name did Jerry have for the B.O. car?

200) What was Sidra, Jerry's girlfriend, referring to when she told him they were "spectacular"?

201) For what reason was George banned from the health club?

202) What is Mr. Benes, Elaine's father's occupation?

203) What's Jerry's explanation for men and women not getting along?

204) What is the most popular food eaten at Jerry's apartment?

205) When George was a kid, who did his friends say his mother was uglier than?

206) What was the name of the lawyer who represented Kramer in his lawsuit against Java Coffee?

207) What settlement was Kramer awarded in the lawsuit with Java Coffee?

208) What was the name of the trenchcoat Jerry's dad invented?

209) What was the special feature of the trenchcoat?

210) What was the name of "Golden Boys," Jerry's favorite teeshirt, replacement?

211) What did Jerry buy his parents that caused them to be kicked out of their retirement development?

212) Who parks cars for the neighbors in Jerry's apartment building?

213) Why did Kramer get fired from the Woody Allen movie?

214) What line did Kramer have in the Woody Allen movie?

215) How does Jerry describe someone becoming gay?

216) What was the name of the waitress at Reggie's diner?

217) Why did George get kicked out of the Soup Nazi's kitchen line?

218) What type of business was Elaine's boss, Mr. Peterman, in?

219) Why does George never carry a pen?

220) Jerry gets audited for contributing to what charity?

Answers

1) Mendy's
2) Brueline
3) Mansiere or The Bro
4) A Christmas Card)
5) Babs
6) The Beach
7) Tweety Bird
8) The Improv and The Comedy Club
9) Frank and Estelle
10) Superman
11) A Black and White Cookie
12) Reggie's
13) Helen and Morty
14) *Tropic of Cancer*
15) Pendant
16) Assman
17) Stella
18) The Parks Department
19) Having Sex with the Cleaning Lady on his Desk
20) Tina Roberts
21) KL5-8383 or KL5-2390
22) A Titlist Golf Ball
23) War! What is it Good For
24) Golden Boy
25) *Regis and Kathi Lee*
26) He did the Opposite
27) A Box of Jujyfruit's Candy
28) Uromisitisis
29) All Tags from 32W to 31W
30) Bosco
31) Kenny Banya
32) $13,000

33) A Junior Baby Label Maker
34) Risk
35) Re-Gifter
36) A Watch
37) Joe Dimaggio
38) It Moved
39) Nothing
40) Maestro
41) The Security Guard had to Stand
42) Kramer, with a Cigar
43) Uma Thurman
44) Love Letters to her Father from John Cheever
45) Klein
46) $10.00
47) Danny Tartabull
48) With a Knife and Fork
49) Latvian Orthodox
50) Fungicide Medicine
51) Hunan Balcony
52) He is a High-Talker
53) He wore a Cape
54) Woody Woodpecker
55) With Newman's Mailbag that Belonged to "Son of Sam"
56) His Houndstooth Sport Jacket
57) He claims Jerry cheated in a Race
58) 16 WEST 75TH STREET, APT. 2G)
59) *Melrose Place*
60) Mutton
61) He sold it to a Sports Memorabilia Store
62) Paul O'Neill
63) George Steinbrenner
64) Martin Van Nostrand
65) A Box of Raisins
66) On A Greenpeace Boat
67) Mr. Seinfeld's Wallet
68) *Sic Semper Tyranus*
69) Vandalay Industries
70) Phillies and Mets 6/14/87

71) 129 EAST 81ST STREET, New York City
72) He smokes
73) Roger McDowell
74) The Soup Nazi's Recipes
75) Queens
76) To wear the "Puffy" Shirt on the *Today Show*
77) Bryant Gumbel
78) George
79) A Mimbo
80) Rock Climbing
81) Erika, the Phone Sex Lady
82) Jorrel
83) Fong
84) Ten Years
85) Walden's
86) Malaysia
87) Newman
88) Mr. Lippman
89) Plyometric, Vertical-Leap Training Shoes
90) *Penthouse* Magazine
91) He had Fleas in his Apartment
92) From Newman
93) When You clean the Bathtub
94) Elaine
95) Marie
96) "You are so Good Looking"
97) Twenty-Five Times
98) Colt .45
99) The Vault
100) *Seinlanguage*
101) Brentano's
102) *Glamour*
103) Gail
104) The Pick
105) Curtis
106) His Trenchcoat
107) *Rochelle, Rochelle*
108) At 44TH and 9TH Avenue

109) Kramer
110) Spinach
111) Mickey Mantle
112) Jon Voight
113) Ping
114) Biff
115) His immigration Renewal Form
116) *Murphy Brown*
117) Skin Moisturizer
118) Fred Savage
119) Lupe
120) Not to tuck in the Sheets
121) "The Keys"
122) *All My Children*
123) Ruthie Cohen
124) Mickey Mantle corking his Bat
125) Harold and Manny
126) He Double-Dipped a Chip
127) A Big Screen Television
128) Hipster Dufus
129) Seinsmelled, Jerry Jerry Dingle Berry
130) A Junior Mint Candy
131) Buck Naked
132) "Having No Hand"
133) *Schindler's List*
134) Rudy's Antique Boutique
135) A Frightened Turtle
136) Enzo
137) High School Equivalency
138) Korean
139) Bette Midler
140) *Rochelle, Rochelle*
141) Their Dad won Money at the Track
142) Buddy
143) Poppie
144) He was Against Abortion
145) Make-Your-Own Pizzas
146) Seomeone Pushed Him into a Hot Iron

147) *Breakfast at Tiffany's*
148) He takes off his Shirt
149) The Clowns
150) Worlds Colliding
151) Ramon
152) Thirty-Seven Times
153) Donald
154) Cuban Cigars
155) Albert Pepper
156) He Claims it Attracts Women
157) Vacuuming
158) Car-Accident Man is Sentenced to be Jerry's Butler
159) Extra MSG
160) Mona
161) *Rochelle, Rochelle*
162) 1990 BMW
163) Steven Snell
164) Baltimore Orioles
165) 1971
166) *I Love Lucy*
167) George Kissed her at a Meeting
168) It was made of Velcro
169) "La Cocina"
170) J.F.K. High
171) To the Cuban Government for Cigars
172) Farfel
173) Underwear
174) Isosceles
175) David Letterman
176) Milanos
177) Manuscript Research
178) $182 in Cash
179) "Shaft"
180) Can't Stand Ya
181) Bugs in the Food
182) Cartwright
183) A Napkin with Jokes on it
184) Cherry Binaca Breath Spray

185) A Chucker
186) 6'3"
187) Magellan
188) Help Him Move
189) Baked Beans
190) Atomic Wedgie
191) Hennigans
192) Pete's Luncheonette
193) Mary Hart
194) Jerry Asked for his Spare Set of Keys Back
195) Her Diaphragm
196) A Kick in the Head by Joe Davola
197) He Has Legs
198) Cosmo
199) The Beast from Hell
200) Her Breasts
201) He Peed in the Shower
202) Novelist
203) God's Plan for Them not to be Together
204) Cereal
205) Television's "Hazel"
206) Jackie Chiles
207) Free Coffee
208) The Executive
209) Beltless
210) Baby Blue
211) A Brand New Cadillac
212) Sid
213) Kramer broke a Glass and a Piece hit Woody
214) "Boy, these Pretzels are making me Thirsty."
215) Changing Teams
216) Hildy
217) He asked for Bread
218) Clothing
219) He's afraid he will puncture his Scrotum
220) Victims of the Krakatoa Volcano